4.95

MW01105311

The n
world famous
scientist

Text copyright © 2002 by Susan Hughes
Illustrations copyright © 2002 by Steven Taylor

Published in Canada by Fitzhenry & Whiteside,
195 Allstate Parkway, Markham, Ontario L3R 4T8

Published in the United States by Fitzhenry & Whiteside,
121 Harvard Avenue, Suite 2, Allston, Massachusetts 02134

All rights reserved. No part of this book may be reproduced in any manner without the
express written consent of the publisher, except in the case of brief excerpts in critical
reviews and articles. All inquiries should be addressed to Fitzhenry & Whiteside
Limited, 195 Allstate Parkway, Markham, Ontario, L3R 4T8

www.fitzhenry.ca   godwit@fitzhenry.ca.

10 9 8 7 6 5 4 3 2 1

National Library of Canada Cataloguing in Publication Data

Hughes, Susan, 1960 – The not-quite world famous scientist

(1st flight) ISBN 1-55041-696-0

I. Title. II. Series: First flight chapter book.

PS8565.U42N68 2002   jC813'.54   C2002-900926-X
PZ7.H87396No 2002

U.S. Cataloging-in-Publication Data
(Library of Congress Standards)

Hughes, Susan.
The not-quite world famous scientist : a first flight level four reader / by Susan Hughes;
illustrated by Stephen Taylor. -- 1st ed.
[93] p. : ill. ; cm. (A first flight chapter book)
Summary: Alexandra Bointon dreams about becoming a scientist, but for the annual
school science fair she is teamed up with a new boy, rather than her best friend.
Dealing with her new and old friends opens her to new challenges.
ISBN 1-55041-696-0 (pbk.)
1. Science Fair -- Fiction. 2. Friends -- Fiction.
I. Taylor, Stephen, ill. II. Title. III. Series.
[F] 21 2002 AC CIP

Fitzhenry & Whiteside acknowledges with thanks the Canada Council for the Arts, the
Government of Canada through the Book Publishing Industry Development Program
(BPIDP), and the Ontario Arts Council for their support for our publishing program.

Design by Wycliffe Smith Design Inc.
Printed in Canada

A First Flight® Level Four Reader

The not-quite world famous scientist

By Susan Hughes
Illustrated by Stephen Taylor

Fitzhenry & Whiteside

To the real Alex, my totally terrific niece.
S.H.

CHAPTER ONE
WHO ME?

The not-quite world famous scientist bent over her test tubes. One test tube contained a dark yellow liquid. It was bubbling and popping. She called it buboolopulous troobulopulous *or "Bubble Trouble." The other test tube contained a murky pink mud. It was gucky and thick. She called it* mukinious gukinious *or "Muck Guck." Purple smoke billowed out from both test tubes.*

The scientist was all set. She was wearing her white lab coat. She was wearing her protective goggles and her protective gloves.

Now it was time.

The not-quite world famous scientist had worked hard for this moment. She had created both test tube mixtures. She had traveled across the country choosing the ingredients. She had mixed them in just the right quantity. When she put the two mixtures together, it could change the world!

Was she nervous? No, nothing alarmed the not-quite world famous scientist—ever. She was always as cool as a cucumber.

Carefully, she picked up the test tube of Bubble Trouble. *Carefully, she picked up the test tube of* Muck Guck.

The not-quite world famous scientist took a deep breath. She was young. She was not-quite world famous. But after this experiment, everyone would know her name. Alexandra Bointon. Everyone would know that Alexandra Bointon was a genius.

Alexandra carefully poured some yellow liquid into the pink muck.

Oh, no! The explosion was enormous!

The test tubes flew out of her hands and into the air.

The test tubes seemed to twirl in slow motion. Sparks flew out of them. The purple smoke turned blue, then pink, and then orange with silver flecks. The smell was horrible!

Did the scientist lose her cool? Did she panic? Not a chance. Even when she saw that the test tubes might smash on the floor and all her work would be lost.

This gal wasn't a quitter. No way. Not her.

The not-quite world famous scientist made a spectacular dive. Hands out-stretched, she leapt toward the falling test tubes.

You had to see it to believe it. It was remarkable.

Just before the test tubes hit the floor, Alexandra Bointon caught them both.

Yes, the not-quite world famous scientist caught the new solution that could change the world and end all disease.

Alexandra Bointon lay on the floor with a test tube in each hand. She had a smile on her face.

Alexandra Bointon had done it again. Alexandra Bointon!

Alexandra Bointon smiled again. What a great feeling. Wasn't being a scientist wonderful...?

Alexandra Bointon!

"Alexandra Bointon!"

Her name would be in all the science journals. Her name would be in all the textbooks in every school around the world.

"Do you hear me, Alexandra?"

Alexandra opened her eyes. She looked up. Mr. Ali, her fourth-grade teacher, was gazing down at her. Mr. Ali shook his head. "Daydreaming again?" he asked.

"Who me?" answered Alexandra. She tried to say it as if it might be funny. But it was never funny to Mr. Ali.

CHAPTER TWO
IN A BAD SPOT

Mr. Ali had his hands on his hips. He was still waiting for Alex to confess to daydreaming. Alexandra's mind was racing. Any minute now she would think of a great excuse.

But Mr. Ali shook his head. He put up his hand like a stop sign.

"Forget it," he said. "I don't want to know. Not this time."

Some of the kids in the class snickered.

"You are the only one who hasn't chosen a partner," Mr. Ali told Alexandra.

She stared up at him, puzzled. A partner for what? she wondered. She didn't dare ask.

Instead, Alexandra shot a look across the room at Teagan. Teagan was her best friend.

She usually picked Alex for a partner. She usually saved Alex from messes like this.

But Teagan was shrugging her shoulders. She was pointing at Frances.

Oh yes, Alexandra remembered. Teagan had told her that the next time there was a project, she really wanted to ask Frances to be her partner. Alex didn't get it. Why would anyone want to choose a science partner who was only interested in fashion?

Teagan had explained that that was exactly why she wanted Frances as a partner. Teagan was interested in fashion too. And she hoped that if she and Frances were partners, they could try on clothes at her house. They could design some outfits together. Maybe Frances would even go window-shopping with Teagan.

Ugh. Alex shuddered at the thought. She just wasn't interested in clothes. And Teagan knew it. That's why she wanted to make a new friend.

Alex knew it was logical. She knew it made sense. So of course Alexandra had agreed that Teagan should ask anyone she wanted to be her partner. Yet, Alex still had to try hard not to feel hurt.

But now what? Who would be her partner?

Alexandra looked around the room at her classmates. Other than Teagan, she really didn't have very many friends.

It turned out it didn't matter much. She wasn't going to have a choice of partners.

Mr. Ali was talking to her again. "Everyone else has buddied up. Except you…and Keith."

Alexandra groaned. Oh no. Don't say it! she ordered Mr. Ali silently. But the thought control didn't work. It never did.

"So you and Keith will be partners," Mr. Ali finished.

Alexandra groaned. "But…" she began.

The bell rang. As all the children began talking, Mr. Ali said in a loud voice, "Now, don't forget. There are only two and a half weeks until the science fair. You should start on your projects right away."

Alexandra groaned again. She buried her face in her hands.

A science project. Her favorite thing in the whole world. Usually she loved doing science projects.

But that was because Teagan was always her partner. Teagan always let Alex choose

what project to do. Alex made all the deci-
sions. Teagan let her organize the work,
and Teagan did just what Alex said. She
was the most perfect partner in the whole
world. Working with Teagan was almost as
good as working alone. The girls really
understood each other.

Keith Parker. He was new. He'd hardly
spoken at all in class yet, and Alex knew
almost nothing about him. Normally Alex
was fine with new kids. She admired them
for starting a new school and making new
friends. It was hard enough making friends
even when you'd been at the same school
all your life.

But Keith...Alex was uncertain about
him. He was definitely a little weird. She
couldn't exactly put her finger on it. Maybe
it had something to do with the fact that he
always had dirt under his nails. *Always.*
Maybe it had something to do with the fact
that he got up about ten times a day to
sharpen his pencil. Make that *twenty* times
a day. And maybe it had something to do
with the fact that, every time Alex walked
by his desk, he quickly stopped working
and covered what he was doing. Did he

think she was going to copy his answers?
Did he think she would cheat?

Yup, these reasons were enough to rule
him out as a partner.

Alexandra decided what she would
do. She would speak to Teagan. *She*
would have to be Teagan's partner.
Frances could be her partner next time.
Teagan wouldn't mind if she knew
what a bad spot Alex was in.

Alexandra looked up. She
saw Teagan across the room. She
packed up her books and was about
to go and catch her.

But she couldn't. Keith was standing
right by her desk, blocking her way.
And then Teagan was talking to
Frances. The two girls left the
room together.

"Hi," said Keith.

"Yeah. Hi," said Alexandra.
"Listen, Keith. About this
project. I need to tell you
something."

Alexandra stood up and grabbed her
books. She looked Keith right in the eye.

"Yeah, I need to tell you something too," said Keith.

He spoke quickly, almost as if he knew what she was about to say. "My aunt is a scientist," he said. "And she may be able to help us. Her name is Karen Tissott."

Alexandra froze. Her eyes opened wide. *Karen Tissott?!* Keith's aunt was *Karen Tissott?!*

She put her books down. Maybe her talk with Teagan could wait.

SHE LIVES ... WHERE?

"Your aunt is Karen Tissott?" Alex said aloud, wonderingly. Keith definitely had her attention. "*The* Karen Tissott?"

Alex couldn't believe it. Just last weekend she'd read an article about Karen Tissott in the latest issue of *Junior Scientist.*

"Um, yeah, I guess so." Keith shrugged. "Aunt Karen is pretty famous, I guess. She teaches and does her own experiments. She's mostly interested in chemistry." Keith rubbed at his ear. There was a yellow blotch of paint on it.

Then Keith paused. He added to himself, "Chemistry? Yeah, I think that's right." His voice trailed off.

Alex fixed him with her best "are you crazy?" stare. "You don't know?" she said suspiciously. "She's a world famous scientist and she's your aunt, and you don't know for sure what she does?"

Keith spoke quickly. "Well, she and I don't talk about science much. And I've really only met her a few times."

"And why is that?" asked Alex.

"She's lived in Australia since before I was born," explained Keith. He jammed his hands in his jeans. Then he took one hand out and scratched again at his ear.

"Oh," said Alex. Her sudden interest in being Keith's partner faded instantly. Karen Tissott might be Keith's aunt, but how could she help them if she lived so far away?

"Keith, I have to go."Alex picked up her knapsack and packed up her books. She stepped around Keith.

"But we should decide when we're going to meet to talk about the project. We need to get some ideas, don't we?" Keith suggested. "Especially since the project's due in two and a half weeks."

"Keith, I'm kind of busy this weekend," Alex said. She shifted the weight of her knapsack. "I've got lots of homework to do.

I have to wash my dog. I have to deliver papers with my sister tomorrow and Sunday. I have to get my skates sharpened. You know. Lots of stuff to do."

Now Alex had the open door in her sights. She could see Teagan talking to Frances and some other friends in the hallway. Teagan was probably waiting for her, like she usually did. Alex and Teagan lived on the same street. They had been neighbors since they were little kids. They had been walking home from school together for years.

Alex took another step away from Keith. She wanted just to say goodbye and leave.

But she couldn't walk away. Something was holding her back, and she knew what it was. It was the scientist in her. The scientist in Alex liked things to make sense. And this didn't. Why would Keith have mentioned his aunt if he knew she couldn't help them?

Alex turned. "Keith, how did you think your aunt could possibly help us with our project if she lives on the other side of the world?"

Keith grinned. "Actually, I've been e-mailing her for years," he said. "Aunt Karen and I don't chat a lot about science, but we talk about lots of other things."

Alex felt herself start to blush. Of course, *e-mail!* Why hadn't she thought of that? Maybe Karen Tissott could help them out through cyberspace after all.

Keith was still talking. "Plus, she's planning to fly in this weekend for a visit. I thought we could get together with her and talk about the project. Is she coming on Sunday? Or is it Saturday?" He stopped and counted on his fingers. "No, it's definitely Sunday."

Alex's face froze. Keith's world famous aunt was arriving *this weekend?*

"But if you're busy... I guess we'll have to wait until next week after all," Keith finished. He rubbed at his ear one last time. This time the yellow paint came off. Keith turned away and started for the door.

Alex didn't say anything for a few seconds.

Then she spoke. "Maybe you're right."

Keith stopped.

"Maybe we should try to get started on this right away. I guess I can wash my dog tonight, and I can do all my homework and get my skates sharpened on Saturday. That way I'll have time to meet with you on Sunday. What do you think?" She held her breath.

Keith shrugged. "Sure," he said. He smiled. "Where do you want to meet?"

"How about your place?" suggested Alex quickly. "Then your aunt will be right there for us to talk to...if we have any trouble or need any suggestions, I mean," she added quickly.

"Okay," Keith nodded. "Aunt Karen is great. I'm sure she'll help us when she gets here."

"Super," said Alex.

"I'll give you my address and telephone number," suggested Keith. He began pulling a piece of paper out of his backpack. "Come over after lunch on Sunday."

"All right," Alex agreed. Keith glanced down at the paper he had found and then hurriedly returned it to his pack, tucking it carefully behind his thick math textbook.

"Uh, sorry," Keith said, with a quick laugh. "Just private stuff."

He turned his back to block her view while he searched awkwardly for a different sheet of paper.

Alex shrugged. She already knew Keith was weird. A little more weird behavior didn't matter. "No problem," she told him. But she wished he'd hurry. She wanted to tell Teagan the great news right away. Keith had a Super Aunt who was a world famous scientist. And Alex was going to meet her!

Keith's face was red as he wrote down the information and handed it to her.

"Great. See you," Alex said, shoving the paper in her pocket. She hurried out of the room to find Teagan.

But her best friend wasn't in the hallway anymore. Teagan had left without her.

Alex sighed with disappointment. Everyone knew that she wanted to be a scientist one day. But Teagan was the only one who knew Alex dreamed of being a *world famous* scientist. Teagan was the only one she could really share her secrets with. And her dreams. She was the only one who would have understood how excited Alex was to meet Karen Tissott.

Alex kicked her way home through the colorful November leaves. Why hadn't Teagan waited another few minutes for her? Maybe Frances had invited Teagan over to her house. But did Teagan really think that trying on clothes was more fun than doing science experiments? Alex knew the answer was yes. Teagan often did science experiments with her just because they were best friends—not because she enjoyed it.

Maybe I should have tried harder to do things that *Teagan* liked doing, Alex thought gloomily.

The sky was gray and there was a chill in the air. Skating season would start soon. The local arena was already offering free family skating on weekends. She remembered how Teagan had finally given up trying to talk her into figure skating lessons. That was probably another reason Teagan wanted to be friends with

Frances. Frances was a devoted figure skater. She spent hours at the rink practising jumps and twirls. She had even won some local competitions.

Alex tried not to care. She told herself that science was more important. Science was more important than anything— especially clothes and figure skating.

When Alex arrived home, Florence was sitting out front on the stoop. As usual, her older sister was wearing black jeans, a black shirt, and a black nylon jacket. She had used tiny elastics to spike her hair in tufts.

There was a huge pile of newspapers and a stack of grocery flyers in front of Flo. She was inserting a flyer into each paper

and then throwing the newspaper into a new pile. Every time she threw one, a small gray schnauzer on a long rope leaped through the air and landed on the growing pile. This made Flo frown.

"Hi, Flo," Alex called. "Hi, Clarkson."

The dog paused in mid-run and turned. He sped to Alex, jumped into her arms, and licked her face.

"Want to help, Alex?" Flo said without looking up.

"Sure, sis," agreed Alex. "I'll be there in a minute."

"Take Clarkson with you," Flo commanded. Then she muttered, "That rope is way too long."

Alex unclipped Clarkson's collar and shifted the dog under one arm. Opening the front door, Alex threw her knapsack in. She called out, "I'm home, Mom. I'm going to help Flo with the papers." She grabbed Clarkson's leash, then shut the door and ran into their small backyard, where she'd set up her mini weather observatory.

Alex took weather observations once a day, and sometimes twice. She was experimenting to see how accurately they could help her predict the weather. So far, the results were quite good.

Alex grabbed the clipboard from the wall of the garage and turned to the current page. Despite Clarkson's wiggling, she managed to fill in the date neatly. Then she checked her rain meter. It was empty. She wrote "zero" under precipitation. She looked at the odometer. The wind was blowing a tiny bit. She recorded the speed. The temperature on the thermometer read, "15 degrees C." She put the correct figure in its place.

Alex shifted Clarkson under her other arm and returned the clipboard to its hook. Then she hurried back into the front yard.

"Okay, Flo," Alex said. Florence didn't say anything, but Alex heard what sounded like a grunt. Florence was sixteen. Until about two months ago, she had talked non-stop. But ever since her birthday, she'd been mostly silent. She would only wear black clothes, and her hair had to be constantly spiky. Alex's parents said not to worry. It was all part of growing up.

Actually, Alex quite liked this new Florence. They seemed to get along a lot better now that they didn't say as much to each other.

With one hand, Alex helped Flo stack half of the assembled newspapers into their wagon. With the other hand, she tried to keep away the excited schnauzer, who was keen on toppling the pile. The frown didn't leave Flo's face, but she didn't complain anymore.

Soon they were ready to head out. Now Alex had Clarkson's leash in one hand and pulled the wagon with the other. Flo delivered the papers from door to door.

Flo worked in silence, but Alex chatted to her anyway. She told her about her upcoming spelling test. She told Flo how much she hated art class. She even told her a little about Teagan's new interest in clothes, figure skating—and Frances. The sisters emptied the wagon and then returned to their house to load up with the remaining papers. This time Flo pulled the wagon and Alex delivered.

"There's a new boy in my class," Alex told Flo as they waited to cross the street. "I have to do a science project with him."

"Hmmm," was Flo's response. She stared straight ahead.

Alex delivered one paper, and then another. Clarkson pulled at the leash, trying to sniff at every blade of grass.

"The boy's name is Keith Parker. He's weird." Alex didn't come right out and ask her, but she hoped that maybe Flo would have some tips about weird boys. Her sister was pretty weird herself these days.

All the teen mumbled was, "Parker, eh? His older sister Leah is in my class."

Not much help, Alex thought to herself, but still, it was more than her sister *usually* said.

They finished delivering the last half-dozen papers, and gratefully returned home. Flo paid Alex her split of the wage right away. Alex let Clarkson off the leash, ran up to her bedroom, and put the money directly into her piggy bank. She was saving for a new microscope. She shook her bank. It sounded quite full.

Alex lay back on her bed. Maybe she could ask Keith's Aunt Karen about microscopes. Maybe Aunt Karen could help Alex choose just the right microscope for her. Maybe she could even help Alex set up some slides....

Suddenly Alex remembered. If she was going to meet Aunt Karen—that is, if she was going to have time to get to Keith's, work on the project, and meet Aunt Karen —she had to wash her schnauzer tonight.

She jumped out of bed, calling, "Clarkson! Here, boy!"

Alex could hardly wait until Sunday.

CHAPTER FOUR
AUNT KAREN'S IDEA

No one thought it could be done. Even Alexandra Bointon, the not-quite world famous scientist, had doubts.

But nothing would stop her from trying the impossible. Nothing!

And now here she stood. In her hands was the first Bointon Oxygen-Powered Battery. Would it work? Could it really power a car? Would humankind be free forever from using gasoline? Or even solar power?

Alexandra Bointon put the Bointon Oxygen-Powered Battery into the car. She hooked it up easily to the special wires. It was a normal car. It could hold four people and a dog. In fact, it was her family's car. She had simply removed the gas tank and the regular battery.

Alexandra Bointon got behind the driver's seat. She was too young to drive, of course. But she had been granted a special licence for this day.

The not-quite world famous scientist put the key in the ignition. She turned the key.

The battery started!

Alexandra shifted the car into drive. She reached down and put her foot on the accelerator.

The car moved.

The car was moving!

Alexandra smiled. Success! Her battery created no pollution. All it needed was oxygen from the air. And it would drive this car forever.

Before Alexandra knew it, she was standing in front of Keith's door. She knocked.

Keith opened the door almost right away. "Hi," he said, smiling.

"Hi," Alex said. She took off her jacket, and Keith hung it up while she untied her shoelaces.

"My mom is upstairs. You can meet her later," said Keith.

"Sure, sure," said Alexandra. "So, is your aunt here yet?"

Alex looked around. The house seemed quiet. Not quite like a relative from Australia had just arrived. And a world famous relative at that.

Keith looked at his watch. "No, she should be here anytime though," he said. "My dad and sister went to pick her up at the airport."

Alex was disappointed. There was a moment of silence.

Then Keith spoke up. "So, let's think of some ideas for the science project."

He led Alex into a room that faced the backyard. There were two bookshelves stuffed with books, some potted plants, and two colorful paintings hanging on the wall. There was a low table and some floppy chairs and lots of windows. "The study is a good place to think," Keith said. "It's my favorite room in the house."

Alex sat down in a beanbag chair and nearly sank up to her neck. She managed to scramble back up to the surface.

"Here's a list of my ideas," she said to Keith. She reached into her bag and handed him a piece of paper.

Keith read over the list. "Making a volcano...Magnet experiments...Plants in a

box..." His eyes moved quickly.

"Pretty good." Keith nodded. He rubbed at his left upper arm. Today he had a green splotch of paint on his left elbow.

"So which one should we choose?" Alex said. "I think making a volcano would be fun. But it's pretty simple. And it's been done lots of times before. Although I could make the volcano out of papier-mâché and paint it."

Keith interrupted, "You mean *we* could make a volcano. This is a project for partners. No marks unless both partners participate."

"Right, right," said Alex quickly. "Making a wind tunnel would be fun too. I...I mean, we...could put a hair dryer at one end and blow air in. And...we...could make several aerofoils and test them to see which one flies best. Or...."

"Don't you want to see my suggestions?" Keith asked.

Alex paused, surprised that Keith had bothered to come up with any ideas of his own, surprised that he would still mention them after hearing her great ideas. When Teagan was her partner, *she* had never made any suggestions. Teagan had always let Alex pick which project to do, and Alex had liked it that way.

But Alex shrugged. "Okay. Sure," she said reluctantly.

Keith handed her a piece of paper.

There were three experiments listed, Alex saw. The ideas were actually quite good.

"I e-mailed Aunt Karen about this project on Friday night," Keith said. "These experiments were her suggestions."

Ahhh, that explains it, Alex thought to herself. She read the experiments again. One experiment combined sugar and water, and one experiment mixed salt and water. The third experiment involved making a "garden" using charcoal briquettes, salt, laundry bluing and water.

"I like them—all three of them," Alex said. She began to get excited. "The first two are simple but interesting. We combine sugar and water to make a solution. We do the same thing with salt and water. We hang a string into each of the two solutions. Then we wait."

"And Aunt Karen doesn't tell us what will happen. She wrote 'In about fourteen days, you'll see a surprise!'" said Keith.

"And the charcoal garden sounds cool," added Alex. "I wonder what it would look like when it's done?"

Suddenly she grinned. "Hey, Keith. Let's

do them all. Let's do all three experiments!"

"All right," he agreed instantly.

The front door opened. Keith jumped up and went into the hallway. Alex moved to the doorway of the study. From there she could see Keith's dad and a teenaged girl come into the house.

Mr. Parker spoke a few words to Keith as he took off his coat, but Alex couldn't hear what he said. Then he waved and called out, "Hello." Alex called back, and Keith's father headed into the kitchen.

The girl hung up her jacket, and now she and Keith were talking too. Then the girl headed toward the staircase.

"Hey there," she said to Alex. The girl turned and looked at Keith strangely, then climbed the stairs.

Keith returned to the study. He gave Alex a small, nervous grin.

"That was my dad, and that was my sister, Leah," he said.

Alex waited, but he didn't go on.

"Where's your aunt?" Alex asked, finally. "Where's your Aunt Karen?"

Keith sat down again. "Oh, well, the flight was delayed," he explained. He spoke in a funny voice. "It seems there was a problem with the airplane. Aunt Karen won't be arriving until Wednesday at about four o'clock."

Alexandra didn't sit down. "Well, it's probably time I got going anyway," she said. She headed for the front door.

As she was putting on her jacket, Keith said, "But when should we set up the experiment? The garden takes about two weeks, remember, and the science fair is two weeks from Thursday." Keith rubbed his left elbow. This time he found the green splotch of paint and peeled it off.

"Um, well." Alexandra hesitated. She finished doing up her buttons. She opened the front door. "How about I get the materials for the experiments...and I come over on Wednesday after school?"

"Okay," agreed Keith.

Alex was about to leave, but something bothered her still. "Leah looked at you so strangely," she pointed out. She waited to see if Keith explained.

Now Keith hesitated. Then he said, "Yeah, well, I don't bring many friends home from school.

I think she was surprised to see you here."

Alex lifted an eyebrow. That did explain the expression on Leah's face. It was probably true. She knew Keith didn't have lots of school friends. And yet....

"See you," Alexandra called over her shoulder.

"Yeah, see you at school," Keith said quickly.

As Alex walked away, she tried to think about the science project. She wanted to try to figure out what exactly would happen if they followed the steps correctly. But her mind was full of questions about Keith instead.

Why did Keith cover up his work when she was nearby? What was he trying to hide? Why did he have such dirty nails? Why was there always a splotch of paint somewhere on Keith? Why did he seem so nervous about his aunt not showing up? Was the famous Karen Tissott *really* going to visit?

Alex frowned, frustrated. She couldn't get the facts to connect. But they seemed to point to one sure thing: Keith had a secret or two.

Not that Alex cared.

CHAPTER FIVE
CRUNCHY PICKLES

It was Tuesday. Alex was trying to eat a sandwich. It wasn't easy—Nosh had just told a great joke, and Alex couldn't stop laughing. She wasn't alone. Mark was rolling his eyes and spluttering a mouthful of milk. Even a giggling Teagan was trying to keep from choking on a carrot.

Alex stopped chewing for a minute. She decided that she would finish the mouthful when she had calmed down.

Then Keith appeared beside their table.

All Alex could do was grimace. Her mouth was full.

"Sit down," offered Teagan before Alex

had time to kick her friend under the table.

"Thanks," said Keith.

It was enough to stop Alex's laughter. She began to chew again. As Keith pulled out a chair, Mark started talking about the Crunchy Pickles.

"It's my favorite band," he explained to Keith. He had a white milk moustache. He licked it off with his tongue.

"Mine too," added Nosh. He picked up his apple. He tossed it from one hand to another. Then he took a huge bite out of it.

"Oh yeah," said Keith casually.

"Who doesn't know the Crunchy Pickles? I have their latest CD. The lyrics are great. Better than their last one." He pulled a giant dill pickle out of his bag and waved it in the air. His fingernails had dirt under them.

"In honor of the Crunchy Pickles, a pickle every day for lunch!" Keith took a loud, crunchy chomp.

"You know the Crunchy Pickles?" cried Mark and Nosh. Their mouths dropped, revealing chewed-up apple in Nosh's open mouth and the last bit of a spring roll in Mark's. "We thought we were their only fans!"

Alex exchanged a pained glance with Teagan. It made her cringe just thinking about the time she had listened to

Mark's Crunchy Pickles CDs. If he weren't her friend, she would have run screaming from the room at the first few notes. She wasn't sure the noise even deserved to be called music.

"Well, now we know they have at least three fans," Keith laughed. "Hey, what's your favorite song?"

"Mine is definitely 'Three Heads are Better than Four'," said Mark. "That part where the guitar goes *nyeh-nyeh-nyehh-hh...*" He began strumming and bobbing his head up and down.

"And what about 'I'd Climb the CN Tower for You—A Step at a Time'," suggested Keith. Suddenly his pickle was a microphone, and he began crooning the lyrics. The other two boys joined in.

Alex finished her lunch quickly, although it was hard to eat and cover her ears at the same time. It seemed like an eternity before they finished the song.

"Well, guys," Alex began. "Do you realize that the temperature has been the same for three days running?"

"How about 'Just Before I Fall Asleep, I Replay that Amazing Goal I Scored in Last

Season's Hockey Game'?" Nosh chimed in. He was about to launch into *that* song when Keith suddenly glanced at his watch.

"Hey, all you Pickles freaks, I have to go," Keith said. Alex breathed a sigh of relief. No more singing.

Keith jumped up. Most of his lunch was still on the table in front of him. He'd been too busy talking and singing to eat. He began putting everything back in his brown lunch bag. "I have a meeting with the principal. She wants to make sure I'm fitting in okay. New school and everything," he added, shrugging.

Then Keith looked at Alex. "By the way, did you get the materials for our project?"

"Oh, not yet," Alex said, startled.

"Want me to come with you and give you a hand?" Keith asked.

"Oh, no. It's okay. I'd rather do it by myself," Alex answered quickly.

"Okay," Keith replied. His bag was packed. "See you later, guys." He gave a wave and walked away.

"Pickles forever," called Mark and Nosh.

Nosh took another huge bite of apple. "Cgee's an cgo-kay cguy," he crunched, nodding.

Alex raised her eyebrows. *Keith's an okay guy.* "Maybe," she said.

Alex turned to Teagan. She wanted to tell her the list of odd things about Keith. She wanted to ask Teagan what she thought about him. But before she could open her mouth, Teagan jumped up. She began frantically packing up her lunch.

"There's Frances," Teagan cried. "I need to talk to her about our science project. See you later, Alex."

Teagan gave Alex a quick wave and hurried across the cafeteria.

Alex sighed. She was definitely on her own.

CHAPTER SIX
WHERE WAS SHE ANYWAY?

"Almost done," said Keith. He worked carefully. He held his tongue between his teeth as he concentrated. The string hanging into the sugar-and-water mixture was a little too long. He was trying to shorten it so the paper clip on the string didn't quite touch the bottom of the jar.

The water had to be hot enough to dissolve the salt and sugar. Keith's mother had insisted on supervising Alex and Keith while they boiled the water and measured it out. Then she had left them alone to finish the experiment by themselves.

Alex glanced at the clock on the kitchen wall. She had been at Keith's house now for half an hour, and he hadn't once mentioned

Aunt Karen. Alex was beginning to wonder why. *Wasn't* Aunt Karen arriving today?

Alex thrummed her fingers on the table impatiently as Keith continued to work on the string. He had dirt under his fingernails, as usual. She'd noticed it about five minutes before—when she had finished hanging *her* paper clip into the salt-and-water mixture. Five *long* minutes ago.

"I like working with my hands. But I'm a bit of a klutz at tying tiny knots," Keith admitted, glancing up for a moment.

"I'll try," Alex offered. She was itching to redo Keith's knot and get on with setting up the garden. What would happen when they combined the materials that Aunt Karen had suggested? She wished that Aunt Karen were there right now. Then she could discuss compounds and chemical reactions. Maybe Aunt Karen would describe some of the amazing experiments she had done. Alex couldn't wait to meet her. Where was she anyway?

"No, no. I want to do it myself," Keith insisted. He went back to his task.

Alex tried to be patient. To distract herself, she wandered over to the paintings on the wall. They were great—loud and splashy with color. They made her feel excited and creative. They made her think of what it would be like to meet Aunt Karen....

"Got it!" Keith exclaimed in triumph. He raised his hands in the air.

"Good," Alex said. She smiled at Keith. He was annoying, but he wasn't a quitter.

Alex immediately returned to the kitchen table. "Now let's get on with the garden," she said enthusiastically.

Alex arranged the charcoal briquettes while Keith measured the water.

"This is the best part of an experiment," Alex said, as she worked. "Setting it all up. Creating the possibilities for...whatever may happen."

Keith nodded. He was concentrating on measuring out the correct amount of salt.

"So, Keith," Alex said casually as she arranged the briquettes in the pan. She just had to ask. She couldn't wait any longer. "No Aunt Karen yet?"

Keith's face turned red. "I know I told you she was going to arrive today," he stammered. "And she did leave Australia. But she was re-routed on her way here."

Keith poured the salt into the water. "There is a world symposium for scientists in France. The key speaker got sick suddenly. They contacted my aunt on the plane and asked her to replace him."

Alex added the liquid bluing to the solution. "Oh," she said flatly. She was disappointed. But not only that, she was suspicious. It seemed too much of a coincidence that Aunt Karen's arrival was delayed again.

Keith spoke quickly. "Aunt Karen e-mailed me from France. She said she was looking forward to seeing us all, but the world of science needed her right away. She said she would come as soon as she could."

"Right," said Alex. She poured the solution on the briquettes.

"But when she gets here, she'll love seeing what we've done," Keith added. "It's a great experiment. Right, partner?" Alex heard the eagerness in Keith's voice. She saw how closely he was watching her face.

Alex forced herself to smile. She didn't want him to know that she thought he was lying. Not until she was sure.

"Yeah," she agreed. "It *is* a great experiment. And this is fun."

But as she added the food coloring to the briquettes, she wondered. Could it be that Keith was making it all up? Could it be that the world famous Karen Tissott wasn't really Keith's aunt after all? She thought back to Keith's dad and Leah returning from the airport. She hadn't even heard what they said when they came in. Maybe they hadn't been to the airport at all! Maybe Keith had made *that* up too!

Alex looked at Keith. There was a lot about him she didn't know. And he was definitely hiding something. But was it this? And if so, why would he lie about having a world famous scientist for an aunt?

CHAPTER SEVEN

SKY SHOWERS

Alex heard the knock at the door. "I'll get it," she called. Not that her sister had moved a muscle anyway. Flo was in her usual nightly pose. She was sitting on the couch with the phone pressed to her ear, giggling and whispering to one of her many weird friends.

Alex flung open the door, sure that the visitor would be Teagan. And she was right.

"Hi, Alex," said Teagan. She was carrying a small pink suitcase.

"Hi!" cried Alex. "I'm so glad you're here. Can you believe it? Can you believe that it's finally November eighteenth, time for the Leonid meteor shower again?" She squeezed her friend's arm excitedly. "You know, the scientists think that North America may get the best meteor shower in thirty-three years!" Alex moved to one side and held her door open wider. "Come on in. We've got to go to bed soon so we can get up before dawn to watch all the action."

But to Alex's surprise, Teagan didn't move. She stayed where she was on the front porch, with the suitcase in her hand. "Alex," Teagan said. "I have something to tell you."

Alex's heart sank. Teagan wasn't smiling. What now?

"I can't watch the meteor shower with you this year." Alex opened her mouth to speak, but Teagan rushed on. "I know we've watched the Leonid shower together every year since we were six. And I know you've been looking forward to it for weeks...*we've* been looking forward to it, I mean...but guess what?" Teagan looked at Alex uncertainly. "Frances invited me and a few other friends to a sleepover at her place tonight."

Alex nodded. "Oh," she said. Why did it have to be tonight? Why couldn't Frances have asked Teagan and her other friends over another night?

"I can't believe it," Teagan was saying. "I'm really sorry it's the same night as the meteor shower. I know you were really excited about it. But I hope you don't mind if I go to Frances' instead."

Teagan looked at Alex hopefully. She clutched the suitcase to her chest.

Alex managed to smile back at her. She tried to feel happy for her friend. She sighed.

"I'll miss you," she told Teagan. "But I know you're not really that interested in studying the sky or the planets or the stars. I hope you have a really good time with Frances."

"Great. Thanks, Alex. You're the best," Teagan breathed. She gave Alex a quick hug. "Let's do something else together this week."

"Sure," Alex agreed. As Teagan hurried away, Alex decided that she and Teagan would still do things together. They would just have to find something they both liked to do. Not watching a meteor shower. Alex was going to be on her own there.

With a sigh, Alex turned to go back into the house. Then she heard a shout.

"Alex! Alex! Wait!"

A dark shape came running up the walk. When it reached the light, Alex saw to her amazement that it was Keith.

"Alex, I've been trying and trying to call

you," the boy panted, "but your phone has been busy forever!" Alex thought of Flo, planted on the couch, the receiver attached to her ear. "I got an e-mail from Aunt Karen just after dinner. She said there might be an amazing meteor shower tonight—well, in fact early tomorrow morning. Before dawn. I was sure you'd want to watch it, so I just had to let you know."

Keith bent over, puffing, his hands on his knees.

Alex's eyes widened with surprise. It was a nice thing for him to do, to run all the way over to her house to tell her. And it made her feel that Karen Tissott likely was Keith's aunt. He wouldn't just make all this up—make up *another* story about an e-mail—would he?

"Well, actually, I *do* know about it already," Alex told Keith. She cocked her head on one side, considering him. "I try to see the Leonid shower every year." She thought about the earth traveling through space. It gave her an excited feeling in her stomach. Her words came out in a rush: "You know, when comets travel too close to the sun, they lose material. They leave a stream of meteoroids along their orbit. If the earth crosses the orbit of a comet—"

"We can see a shower of meteors," put in

Keith. "Aunt Karen wrote that. It's cool." He was still breathing hard, but now he was standing up again.

Alex nodded. "A comet named Tempel-Tuttle orbits the sun every thirty-three years. Every year, the earth passes through its trail. This meteor shower seems to come from the constellation Leo, the lion. So that's why it's called the Leonid meteor shower."

"It happens every November?" asked Keith.

"Yeah," Alex nodded. "But each year is different. And around every thirty-three years, just after the comet passes by, the trail is really dense. Then we might see thousands of meteors!" It gave her the shivers just thinking about it.

"That's what Aunt Karen meant. Amazing." Keith shook his head in awe. "So, are you going to watch?"

"Of course," Alex answered, seriously. "I do every year, and I wouldn't miss this year for anything."

There was a pause. Keith looked like he was about to say something. He opened his mouth. But then he shut it again.

"Alex, you'd better come to bed if you're getting up at 4:45 a.m!" Alex heard her mother call from the kitchen.

"You're getting up at 4:45 a.m.," echoed Keith. "Wow, that's early."

"Yeah," agreed Alex. She shifted from foot to foot. "So I guess I better—"

"Hey, listen," Keith blurted out. He was looking down at his running shoes. "Can I come back? At five this morning, I mean? Can I come and watch the meteor shower with you?"

Alex's mouth dropped open. "Are you sure?" she said. "Are you sure you really want to?"

"Yeah," Keith said. Now he lifted his eyes and looked at her. "Aunt Karen said it shouldn't be missed."

"Well, okay," Alex said, with a shrug. She couldn't help it. Part of her was pleased. She had never watched a meteor shower alone, and now she wouldn't have to. "I'll be in the backyard. I'll put out another lawn chair for you."

"Great," Keith grinned. And before she knew it, he had whirled around and run away.

* * *

When Alex's alarm clock went off at 4:45, she crawled sleepily out of bed and pulled on her clothes. She crept downstairs, holding her sleeping bag. She used her flashlight to find the recliners she had placed in the middle of the back lawn.

Alex had just settled into her seat, when she heard a car slow and stop on the street. In a moment came the sound of a car door closing.

"Okay, son?" came floating through the still, cold air.

Alex heard Keith unlatching her back gate. She shone the beam of her flashlight onto the grass to guide Keith toward her.

"Yes, Dad," called out Keith towards the street. "I'm fine."

Keith crossed the lawn and sank into the recliner beside her. "Hi, Alex," he whispered. "Brrrrr." He hurriedly tucked his own sleeping bag around himself.

Alex turned out her flashlight. "Let your eyes adjust to the darkness for about fifteen minutes," she suggested.

The children lay side by side in silence. Fifteen minutes passed.

"Okay," she said, and they both looked up.

Almost immediately, Alex saw them. Streaks of light falling toward earth. One here, one there. Then, after a few minutes, several here and several there.

"Amazing," breathed Keith quietly.

As Alex watched, the sky became bright with falling meteors. It was truly like being

in a shower of light. She had seen the
Leonids before, but there had never been
such a wonderful show as this.

"Fantastic," she sighed happily.

For the next half-hour, the shower continued. Hundreds of lights rained down. It
was dazzling. Once or twice, Alex had to
remind herself to breathe.

Then gradually, the sky wasn't so dark

anymore. The meteors were more and more difficult to see.

"Dawn's coming," Keith said softly, breaking the silence.

"Yes," Alex agreed sadly. And then finally, morning had arrived.

Alex lay without moving for some time. Her fingers were cold, and so was her nose. But she couldn't quite bear to move from her recliner. She couldn't quite bear to go inside yet.

She turned to Keith. Now it was light enough that she could see his face. "It was like magic," she said, struggling to put her feelings into words. "But it wasn't magic."

He nodded. "You're right," he agreed. "It was better than magic. It was real. It was better than anything."

Alex smiled. Keith had his secrets. And he was certainly weird. But maybe he actually understood how she felt.

Maybe it was okay that he had watched the meteor shower with her.

CHAPTER EIGHT
A PUZZLE SOLVED

The not-quite world famous scientist held the seeds in her hand. It had taken years of experimenting to grow these special wheat seeds. She had worked in the lab. She had worked in the fields. She had grown many other strains of seeds. All had been failures.

And now there were these ones.

The not-quite world famous scientist stood in the hot desert sun. Several months ago, she had marked off a large section of desert. She had taken a breath ... and scattered handfuls of the special wheat seeds. They had fallen here and there on the dry land. Some had fallen in cracks and some had remained on the surface of the parched land.

The hot sun had beaten down on the seeds.

The scientist had turned and walked away. Had she watered the seeds? No. She had simply turned and walked away.

And now she was back. And she was looking across a patch of land full of towering stalks of wheat.

The not-quite world famous scientist smiled. The seeds felt good in her hands. This new strain of wheat didn't need rain. This new strain of wheat would help people grow food in harsh conditions around the world.

Alex arrived at Keith's front door, still smiling from her daydream.

"Hey, Alex," Keith greeted her. "Come on in. I moved the experiments into the study so no one would disturb them."

Alex hadn't seen the experiments since they had set them up last Wednesday. She was anxious to see how the solutions were changing and what was happening in the charcoal garden.

As they entered the room, Alex's eyes went straight to a table near the window where the bottles were set up in a neat row. She hurried toward them.

But suddenly Keith pushed in front of her. He went directly to another table and quickly picked up the sheet of paper that was lying there.

"Be right back," he said without looking at her. And he left the room.

Alex hesitated. What was Keith hiding? She reminded herself that Keith wasn't really her friend. He was only her science partner...and a very strange guy with dirt under his nails and paint dabs always here and there. But yet, it hurt her to know that he was still hiding things from her.

Alex tried to shrug it off. She sat down and began to examine the first experiment.

"Wow!" Alex's eyes widened as she gazed at the first jar. The sugar was beginning to form on the thread. It was separating from the water.

She was looking at the second jar when Keith returned. He seemed a little embarrassed, but he didn't mention the hidden paper. And Alex decided not to ask.

"The experiments look great, don't they?" he offered.

"Yeah," Alex agreed. "The salt is forming on the thread here—just like the sugar is doing in the first jar. Cool!"

"And just look at the charcoal garden," Keith said. He pointed to the shallow tray, and Alex noticed that he had a streak of orange on his wrist. "The charcoal is being

eaten away. The solution is changing it into strange and weird shapes."

"Just like a real garden," Alex pointed out. "Isn't it amazing how you can put two or three materials together and—poof! They create something new."

She crossed her arms and rested her chin on them. As she stared happily at the garden, she forgot her worries about Keith. There were secrets contained in simple things, like charcoal and bluing. Put them together this way or that, and who knew what you might discover? That's what she loved about science.

She remembered her daydream. Without stopping to think, she told Keith about it. She described the whole thing, from beginning to end, while Keith listened.

"And this new kind of seed could grow in any soil, rain or not," she finished. "I was the scientist who invented this terrific seed! What a great daydream!"

Alex looked at Keith. Suddenly she wondered if she'd made a mistake in telling him. Was he going to laugh now?

But he said seriously, "Maybe you really *will* do amazing experiments and invent new things. It'd be hard work, but I bet you could do it."

Alex smiled with relief. "I've always wanted to know how things work and why," she confided. "I've always wanted to make new things—new concoctions, new materials, new tools."

She sat back in her chair. Should she tell him more? Even though he wasn't exactly a friend? Even though he was still keeping secrets from her?

Alex snuck a look at Keith. He seemed to be waiting for her to continue. So she went on, "I've made a weather station outside my house. And you know I like watching meteors."

Keith nodded.

"Well, I have binoculars for watching the stars, too. The walls of my room are covered with charts about chemicals and insects. And my dog Clarkson and I explore the ravine for interesting plants and birds."

Then Alex paused. She looked at Keith curiously. "You don't think that it's strange to be so crazy about something?"

Keith was picking at the dirt under his fingernails. "Actually," he said slowly, "I know just how you feel because there's something *I'm* a bit crazy about too."

"What is it?" Alex said at once.

"Art," he admitted. "Just like you said, I've always wanted to make new things too. Pictures, sculptures, things that I can see. Things that I can imagine."

Alex was surprised. "Can I see some of your work?" she asked.

Keith hesitated for a minute. Then he said, "Sure. Why not?"

He disappeared from the room. Almost as quickly he returned, holding a tray. On it were four sculptures.

Keith carefully set down the tray. Alexandra saw that two of the clay sculptures were horses. One horse was rearing. The second horse was grazing, its head down. The other sculptures were also animals. One was a running dog. The other one was a napping cat.

"These are really great," Alex said. She was surprised. The sculptures weren't perfect. They didn't look *exactly* like real animals. The horse's legs were a bit uneven. And the cat's whiskers were a bit too thick. But oddly enough, these details didn't seem to matter. The animal sculptures had the *feeling* of aliveness. How did Keith do it? Alex wondered. Perhaps it was the way he had the horse's tail snap in the wind, or the way he had made the dog's ears flap.

Keith had vanished again. But when he returned this time, he handed her some thick sheets of paper.

Alex's mouth dropped open as she stared at three oil paintings. One was of a house on a hill. Another was of a sunset. One more was a happy swirl of bright colors.

Alex turned to Keith suddenly. "Those paintings on your walls. Did you paint them?" she asked.

"Yes," said Keith proudly. "My mom and dad framed them and put them up. They really think they're great."

"I think they're great too," Alex said quickly. And she really meant it.

Then she looked at more of Keith's work—three beautiful charcoal sketches of the sugar and salt crystals.

"These are beautiful!" Alex cried. "Almost magical. Hey, why don't we use these in our project? They can be part of our display."

Keith beamed. "Sure," he agreed.

Alex gazed at the sculptures and the paintings. Clay. And charcoal. And the oil paint. Of course.

"I get it," she said aloud. "All this explains your dirty fingernails and the splotches of paint on you. Right?"

Keith blushed and nodded his head. "I try to stay clean, but...I spend so much of my spare time mucking around..." His voice trailed off.

"Hey, it's no big deal," Alex said quickly. "I understand completely." She could tell she had embarrassed him by mentioning the clay and paint marks. She wanted to make Keith smile again.

And he did.

"Just wait until Miss Holmes, the art teacher, discovers you," Alex went on. "She'll be thrilled to find someone who likes art as much as she does."

Keith smiled even more. "You know, it's something I take really seriously," he said. "I can't wait to get home and start in on a new painting or a new sculpture. Sometimes I have to work on an idea for a long time before I get it just the way I want it. Sometimes my family says I spend too much time working on my art and not enough time with my friends."

Alex picked up the sculpture of the dog. "You know, this looks a lot like Clarkson," she told Keith.

"I'd love to meet him sometime," Keith said.

Alex laughed. "If you don't mind slobbery dog kisses, come over anytime!" she said. "And you can see my weather station and look through my binoculars, too."

Suddenly Alex looked at her watch. "I better head home for dinner," she said.

Alex was halfway out the door when Keith suddenly hit his head with the heel of his hand. "Hey, I almost forgot," he said. "Aunt Karen! She's arriving on Saturday evening. She's never been to the Science Center. In fact, no one in my family ever has! So my mom and sister and I are planning to take her there on Sunday afternoon. Do you want to come with us?"

Alex hesitated. There he was, mentioning Aunt Karen again. Was Karen Tissott really Keith's aunt? Alex just didn't know what to believe. It was weird that he kept promising she would show up, and then she

never did. And yet she was sending him
e-mails...*Or was she?* Keith could easily
be finding that information on his own.
But why would he?

Alex's head spun with conflicting
thoughts. He had finally told her about his
art, and she thought she had figured him
out. But there was still this Aunt Karen
stuff....

Alex shrugged. "You bet. Thanks," she
said. "See you tomorrow at school." She
gave Keith a wave as she headed down the
walk. The Science Center was her favorite
place of all. She'd never turn down an invitation to go there.

Even if the invitation came from someone who just might, for whatever weird reason, be making up an aunt.

CHAPTER NINE
NO EXPLANATIONS WANTED

When Keith knocked on Alex's door on Sunday, the first words out of his mouth were, "Aunt Karen isn't here."

Alex just lifted her eyebrows. She wasn't a bit surprised. And in a way, it was a relief. Finally it seemed to confirm that Aunt Karen was a figment of Keith's imagination and not the world famous Karen Tissott that Alex admired.

"Let me explain," Keith began, as they walked to the car.

Alex put up her hand. "Forget it," she interrupted Keith. She didn't want him to make up any more excuses. Alex could see

Mrs. Parker at the wheel of the car. Leah was sitting beside her. She was looking at Keith in that same odd way that she had when she and Keith's dad were supposedly coming back from the airport to get Aunt Karen.

And then suddenly, it struck Alex. She thought about all the facts. She thought about Keith casually mentioning that his Aunt Karen was the famous Karen Tissott. He had done that *after* he knew Alex didn't want to be his science partner. She thought

about him saying that Aunt Karen would be at his house—*after* he figured out that Alex didn't want to come to his house. And she thought about him saying that Aunt Karen would be coming to the Science Center too.

Could it be that he had told all these white lies to keep her interested in being his science partner? Or...Alex got a funny feeling in her stomach. *Could it be that Keith lied because he* liked *her and wanted to spend more time with her?* Alex gulped. That would also explain Leah's funny looks.

Both conclusions were objective. Both conclusions were logical. But they made Alex feel uncomfortable. She didn't want to think about *either* of them right now.

"But—," Keith began again.

"It really doesn't matter why," Alex interrupted him quickly. She really didn't want him to say one word more. Not yet. Not until she had a chance to think through her hypotheses alone. "Let's just forget about it and have a fun time today."

Keith looked surprised and a little relieved. And he didn't say anything more about Aunt Karen the whole afternoon.

When they arrived at the Science Center, Alex flashed her membership card to the ticket taker.

"Hey, Alex," the woman in uniform said with a smile. "Back again?"

Keith grinned at Alex. "You come here a lot, I guess."

Alex nodded.

Keith and Alex agreed to meet Keith's mom and sister at the front entrance in two hours.

"You'll be all right on your own? You won't get lost?" asked Mrs. Parker, seriously.

Alex and Keith shook their heads. Alex tried not to giggle. The Science Center was big, but she knew it like the back of her hand. She just hoped that Keith's mom and sister didn't get lost!

The two hours sped by. There were so many things that Alex wanted to show Keith. Alex and Keith started off at the electricity exhibits. They watched the demonstration of the Van de Graff Generator. A vertical conveyor belt inside a pillar carried negative charges away from the metal ball that sat on top of it. Keith offered to be a volunteer. When he touched

the ball, it took negative charges from his body. The positive charges left over began to push apart...and his hair stood straight out! Alex laughed. It looked like Keith had seen a ghost.

She and Keith walked through the rain-forest room. Hot and sticky in the humidity, they leaned over the hanging bridge to watch the waterfall.

Then Alex and Keith touched all kinds of rocks and minerals and looked at them through microscopes. They watched a short film on a hurricane.

In another room, they marked on a piece of paper what they ate in a day. They inserted the paper in a slot, and comments on their diet slid out.

Finally, they jumped on a "car" powered by jet-air propulsion. It was tricky to try to steer it onto the red crosses marked on the floor.

Then Keith looked at his watch.

"Agh," he groaned. "Time to meet Mom and Leah."

Alex was surprised. "Already?"

"Hey, don't worry," Keith said, as they headed for their meeting spot. "Maybe we can come back again next weekend."

"Nope," Alex said, shaking her head.

Alex saw a look of disappointment on Keith's face, so she continued quickly. "Nope. Next week we go to the art gallery, and you can show *me* around."

THE *SCIENCE* FAIR

The science fair evening was turning out to be a huge success. The school cafeteria had been transformed into a giant display area. Each class in the school had several displays set up.

Alex caught sight of Mr. Ali. He was beaming proudly. On Monday Mr. Ali had announced the three projects that would represent their class in the fair. When he read out Alex and Keith's names, Keith had pumped his fist into the air and cried, "Yes!" Alex had started grinning—and hadn't stopped since.

Now Alex listened as Keith explained to

a parent how they had created their science display. "Well, first we boiled some water. We added sugar to it and stirred."

The woman nodded, listening carefully. Another parent looked closely at the charcoal garden and then read their description of how it was made.

Suddenly Teagan was standing next to Alex. "Great work, Al!" she said, punching her friend lightly on the arm. "Although I wasn't too surprised when your project was chosen to be in the fair."

"It's not just my project. Keith and I shared all the work," Alex corrected her. "But thanks. It turned out really well, didn't it?"

Teagan nodded. "And Keith's drawings of the crystals are great," she added.

Alex had persuaded Keith to pin his drawings to their display board. It added a magical touch to their scientific presentation.

"Want to come over tomorrow after school?" Teagan called over her shoulder as she turned to go.

"Sure," Alex agreed with a smile. She knew they would think of something fun to do together.

A few minutes later, Keith and Alex had a chance to speak.

"This is the first time that someone hasn't been here asking us questions," said Keith. He pushed his hair out of his eyes. Alex saw a pink splatter of paint on his wrist, and she smiled.

"Yeah," Alex agreed. "You know, we really did a great job. We made a good team."

"Real partners," said Keith.

"And we did it without too much help from your Aunt Karen," teased Alex.

Keith was about to speak, but Alex interrupted him. "Since our trip to the Science Center on Sunday, I have decided, once and for all, that Aunt Karen does not exist. Karen Tissott exists, of course. She really is a world famous scientist. But Karen Tissott is not your aunt." She went on calmly. "There is no Aunt Karen. Aunt Karen is a figment of your imagination. The e-mails were clever, but you sent them to yourself, didn't you?"

Again, Keith opened his mouth. But Alex didn't give him a chance to answer.

"Hey, it's okay," she said. "I think I know why you made it all up." Alex blushed. She hadn't been able to decide whether he'd been trying to keep her as a science partner or spend more time with her. She *had* decided it didn't really matter. In either case, she could forgive Keith. "Just no more lies, okay?"

She put out her hand to shake on it. But to her surprise, Keith didn't put out his hand in return.

Before she could ask him why, she heard Mrs. Parker's voice. "There you are, Keith and Alexandra! We're so proud of your work," she said.

Alex turned to thank her.

"What a great job you've done, you two," said a woman beside Keith's mother. The woman suddenly reached out and grabbed Alex's hand, which was still extended. "I'm Aunt Karen," she said. "Keith has told me so much about you. I hope we can spend some time together during my visit."

Alex was in heaven. Since the science fair, she had spent lots of time with Keith and Aunt Karen.

One night Alex had gone for dinner at Keith's house. She and Aunt Karen had talked about chemistry that night. And last night, Keith and Aunt Karen had come to Alex's house for dinner. Keith and Aunt Karen had toured Alex's room and admired her weather station. Clarkson had given them both big slobbery kisses. Yes, it turned out that Aunt Karen liked big slobbery dog kisses as much as Keith did.

And, surprise of all surprises, Flo spoke

to Alex before bed that night.

Alex jumped. She nearly sprayed toothpaste all over the bathroom. Silent Flo was speaking to her! Flo never spoke anymore.

"What did you say?" Alex spluttered, wiping toothpaste off her chin.

"I said, I knew all along that Aunt Karen was real," Flo repeated.

Now the toothpaste was really spraying. "Why didn't you tell me? Why didn't you tell me you knew Aunt Karen was real?" Alex cried. The toothpaste was on the mirror, on the floor, on her pyjamas. "And how did you know that anyway?" she demanded.

Flo looked at Alex. She put her hands on her hips. "Question number two: Leah is in my class and we talk together every day. By the way, she said she was really surprised to see you the day she and her dad tried to pick up her aunt at the airport. Keith hardly ever has friends over."

Alex caught her breath. So *that* was the explanation for Leah's funny looks at Keith!

"And question number one: You never asked me," Flo shrugged, and she went to bed.

Alex sighed. Then she began to clean up

the toothpaste mess.

The next day was Saturday. Alex, Keith, and Aunt Karen spent the morning at the art gallery. Keith showed Alex and his aunt his favorite paintings and sculptures. They finished off in a hands-on room where Alex had fun building a bridge with interlocking blocks while Keith did some pencil sketching. Then she and Keith worked together on a magnetic jigsaw puzzle of a Picasso painting. Finally they joined Aunt Karen in painting on slides.

"Look at this," Aunt Karen marveled. "We can project our masterpieces onto the walls."

And the fun continued.

After a quick lunch, Aunt Karen took Keith and Alex to the local university. She knew some of the science professors there. A professor took the three of them on a tour of the labs. Alex even got to put on a lab coat and protective goggles and mix some chemicals together in real test tubes. It was like a dream come true.

Exhausted, they returned to Keith's house in the afternoon. As they munched on peanut butter cookies, Aunt Karen began telling Keith and Alex about the world symposium in France. Alex sat spellbound as Aunt Karen described some of the up-to-date research that the other scientists had presented.

But when Alex finally managed to drag her eyes away from Aunt Karen and glance at Keith to see his reaction, she giggled. Keith's head was tilted to one side, and his eyes were closed. He was sound asleep.

Alex and Aunt Karen talked on and on, but then Alex finally forced herself to admit, "It's time for me to go home for dinner. My parents feel like they haven't seen me in days."

Keith's mom overheard. "I'll drive you home, dear," she offered.

As Alex stood to go, Aunt Karen asked with a smile, "I have to travel to Kenya soon. Perhaps we'll get together again tomorrow—if that's okay with Keith and the family."

Keith had just wakened from his nap. Stretching and rubbing his eyes, he looked from Aunt Karen to Alex. "If what's okay?" he mumbled.

But his mother nodded. "That would be great!" cried Alex, throwing her arms up into the air. Then, she couldn't help it. She ran up to Aunt Karen and gave her a hug.

"Okay, I think I should take you home now, Alex," said Mrs. Parker. "I'll just get the car keys."

"I'll come along too," Keith suggested.

As Alex went to get her jacket, Keith quickly headed up the stairs. He was back and waiting by the time his mother had found her keys.

The drive to Alex's house was short. In the car, Keith pulled a piece of paper out of a file holder, which he had been hiding in his jacket.

"Here," he said, handing it to Alex.

"What is it?" asked Alex, puzzled. Keith had a funny look on his face.

Then she looked at the paper and her mouth dropped open. It was a picture of her. A beautiful pencil drawing. It was just like her. Maybe not her exact mouth or nose, but...it was just like her.

"Who...?" Alex began. "You drew this?"

Keith nodded. "I started it in class. It took me a long time. I didn't want you to know. I wanted it to be a surprise. You kept trying to look every time you walked by my desk. And then I brought it home and you nearly saw it in the study. It was hard to keep it hidden."

Alex's mouth opened even wider. The last secret had been solved. The last puzzling question about Keith was answered.

"It's really great," Alex managed to blurt out. "Can I keep it?"

"You bet," Keith said with a grin.

The car pulled up in front of Alex's house. She hopped out and thanked Mrs. Parker for the ride.

Before walking off, she stuck her head in the backseat window. "Hey, Keith. I hear

there's going to be an art project assigned next week. Would you mind having a not-quite-great-at-art science lover as a partner?" she asked.

Keith laughed. He stuck out his hand through the window. "Sure thing," he said.

Alex slapped his hand with hers in a high-five, and grinned.

"Partners," they both said firmly.

These are the three projects that Alex and Keith did for the Science Fair. Why not try them yourself? Ask an adult to help you set up.

Making Sugar Crystals

Use a 2-cup (500 ml) glass measuring container or a large drinking glass. Pour in:

1/3 cup (75 ml) boiling water

2/3 cup (150 ml) sugar

Stir in the sugar until all the particles dissolve and you have a thick syrup.

Tie a piece of string to the middle of a pencil. Tie the other end to a clean paper clip. Wet the string and paper clip. Brush them through dry sugar so that grains of sugar stick to them. Place the pencil across the rim of the glass so that the paper clip is suspended midway in the solution.

Cover the glass with a paper towel to keep out the dust—and don't disturb it! After several days, crystals will form around the paper clip and string. If the water evaporates slowly, the crystals will be quite large.

You can eat this sugar candy—but don't eat the string!

Making Salt Crystals

Use a 2-cup (500 ml) glass measuring container or a large drinking glass. Pour in:

1/2 cup (125 ml) boiling water

1/4 cup (60 ml) salt

Stir to dissolve. Some salt grains will still remain.

Follow directions for **Making Sugar Crystals**.

Making a Crystal Garden

Scatter several small pieces of charcoal briquette in a shallow, glass baking dish. Combine:

1/4 cup (60 ml) salt

1/4 cup (60 ml) liquid laundry bluing or whitener (not bleach)

1/4 cup (60 ml) hot water

Stir to dissolve.

Pour the solution over the charcoal briquettes, but don't cover the charcoal completely. You should be able to see the charcoal sticking up out of the mixture. Put several drops of food coloring over the briquette pieces. Place the container where it won't be disturbed.

In a few weeks you'll have a colorful crystal garden. The crystals are fragile, so don't move the container. (Alex and Keith did. They took their garden to school, and because they were *really* careful— and this is fiction—their garden was okay. But in real life, this could have ruined their experiment.)

Don't taste these crystals.